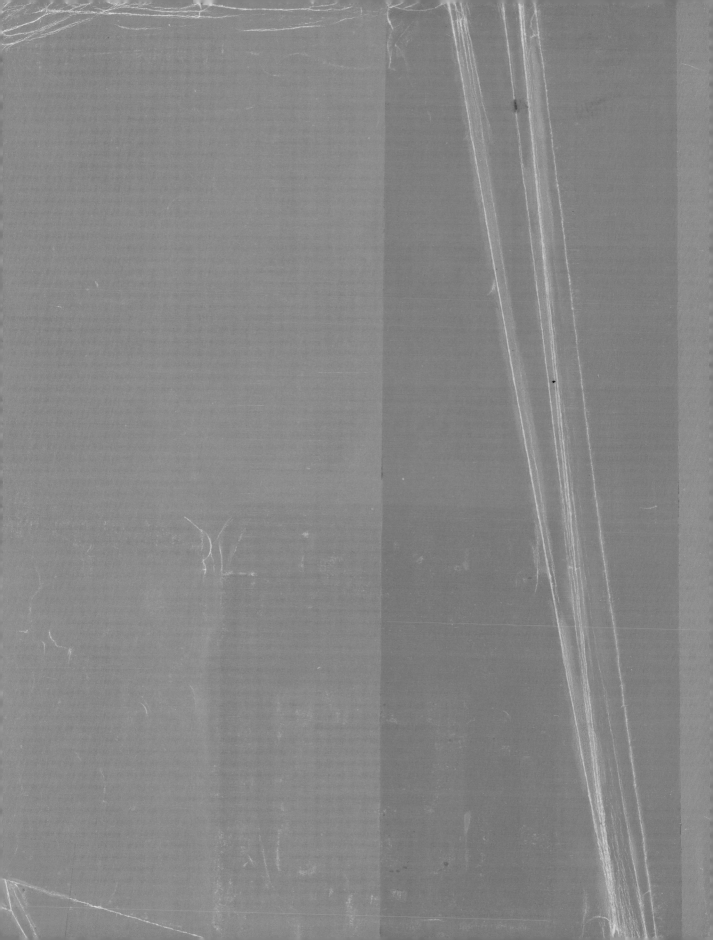

Where Are You Going, Little Mouse?

by Robert Kraus

pictures by **Jose Aruego**
and **Ariane Dewey**

 Greenwillow Books, New York

Text copyright © 1986 by Robert Kraus
Illustrations copyright © 1986 by Jose Aruego and Ariane Dewey
All rights reserved. No part of this book may be reproduced or
utilized in any form or by any means, electronic or mechanical,
including photocopying, recording or by any information storage
and retrieval system, without permission in writing from the Publisher,
Greenwillow Books, a division of William Morrow & Company, Inc.,
1350 Avenue of the Americas, New York, NY 10019.
Printed in the United States of America
First Edition   10   9   8   7   6

The artwork was prepared as black pen-and-ink
line drawings which were combined with full-color
paintings. The typeface is Avant Garde Gothic.

Library of Congress Cataloging in Publication Data

Kraus, Robert, (date)
Where are you going, little mouse?
Summary: A little mouse runs away from home to find a
"nicer" family, but when darkness comes, he misses
them and realizes how much he loves them.
1. Children's stories, American. [1. Mice—Fiction.
2. Runaways—Fiction]   I. Aruego, Jose, ill.
II. Dewey, Ariane, ill.   III. Title.
PZ7.K868Wh 1985   [E]   84-25868
ISBN 0-688-04294-5   ISBN 0-688-04295-3 (lib. bdg.)

For Bruce,
Billy,
Pamela,
Mary Anne,
and
Parker
—R. K.

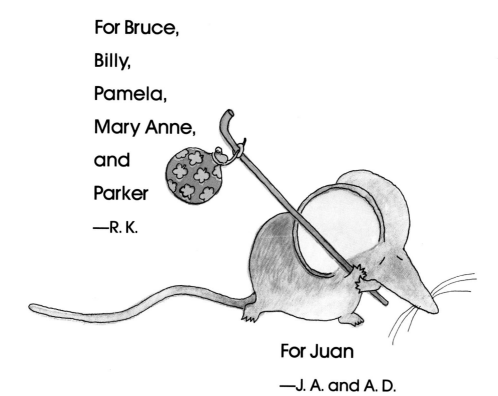

For Juan

—J. A. and A. D.

Where are you going, little mouse?

As far from home as I can go.

What of your mother?
What of your father?

What of your sister?
What of your brother?

They don't love me.
They won't miss me.

What will you do?

Find a new father who plays with me.

Find a new mother who stays with me.

Find a new brother who isn't mean.

Find a new sister.
We're a team.

I'm still looking...
I miss my mother.

I'm exploring...
I miss my father.

I'm still searching...
I miss my sister.

I'm still trying...
I miss my brother.

It's getting dark.
What will you do?

Make a phone call.

Mother, Father,
please don't worry.
Come and get me.
Hurry, hurry.

By the way
they kiss and hug me,
I can tell
they really love me.
I love them, too.

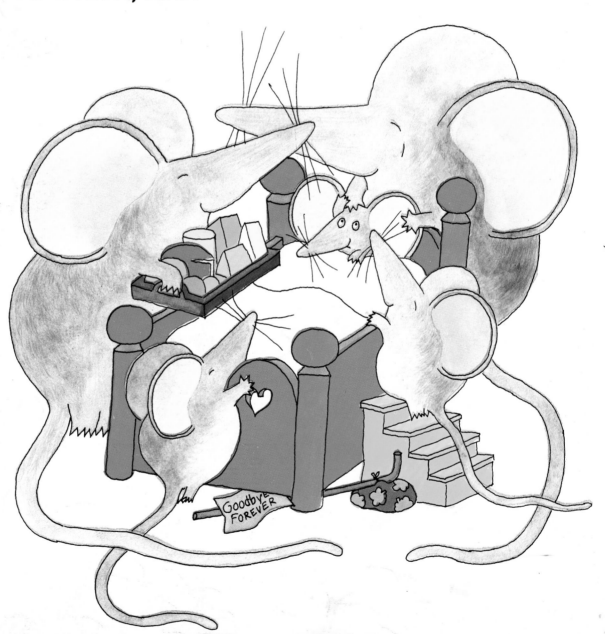